The Moonlight Bride

Also by Buchi Emecheta

Children's Fiction
The Wrestling Match

Novels
In the Ditch
Second-Class Citizen
The Slave Girl
The Bride Price
Double Yoke
The Joys of Motherhood
The Rape of Shavi
The Family

The Moonlight Bride

BUCHI EMECHETA

George Braziller • New York

Library of Congress Cataloging in Publication Data
Emecheta, Buchi.
  The moonlight bride.

  Summary: Two Nigerian girls overhear some elders making
secret preparations for a marriage.
  [1. Marriage—Fiction. 2. Nigeria—Fiction]
I. Title.
PZ7.E575Mo 1983   [Fic]   82-17816
ISBN 0-8076-1062-3
ISBN 0-8076-1063-1 (pbk.)

Printed in the United States of America
Third Printing, 1995

Published in the United States in 1983 by George Braziller, Inc.

Originally published in Great Britain by Oxford University Press
in association with University Press Limited, Oxford House, Iddo
Gate PMB 5095, Ibadan, Nigeria

© *Copyright Oxford University Press, 1980*

The Moonlight Bride

The afternoon of that day was very hot and sunny. So dry was it that all the footpaths leading to each different hut in our cluster of homesteads cracked as if baked in an open fire. The leaves around the bush paths all hung low, looking tired with the heat and brown with the powdery dust that rose and fell with the little wind that blew. There were not many people walking about, and those that were out clustered in small groups under the coconut palms or mango trees or in the shades of their thatched huts.

I leaned against the tall palm tree in front of my mother's hut. I stared for a while at nothing in particular, and feeling very uncomfortable with the prickly heat rashes on my back, I started to rub it against the rough surface of the trunk of the tree. I so enjoyed this roughness against my rash-covered back, that I closed my eyes and went up and down, up and down. I would stop occasionally to work the hollow of my back against the bark of the tree. Then I would close my eyes again and start to go up and down, down and up.

So preoccupied with my enjoyment was I, that I was dead to all the world. Near my mother's hut a group of young men were busy cutting and trimming each other's hair, whilst talking in low lazy voices. Their voices floated to me once in a while, but I was not interested in their problems. On the other side of the footpath was Ogugua's mother's hut. Ogugua's mother stood by her doorway, picking her teeth as usual and spitting out the saliva from her mouth and talking at the same time. This time she was talking to Nwasiwe's mother. I opened my eyes several times to look at these groups of my relatives, but they were always in the same position as before. They seemed to be standing still with the intense sun that was beating directly down on our heads; they seemed to be standing still with the still air. All was so hushed, but for the low murmuring of their voices, and me with my up-and-down movement.

Then all of a sudden a voice shouted into my ear:

'Hi, daydreamer!'

I let out a low cry in alarm. I was not expecting anybody; I did not know that I was being watched by any of my relatives. I had thought that they were all busy minding their business on this hot Eke market-day afternoon. I held my hand to my chest and looked disapprovingly at my cousin and best friend, Ogoli.

'You scared me, Ogoli. I thought you were a ghost. I was almost running away.'

My cousin burst out laughing. She was enjoying it. And she told me how she had been watching me, and how she had managed to conceal herself at the other side of my mother's hut, only jumping at me when she knew I had closed my eyes again.

I did not enjoy hearing this, and even though I had recovered from my initial shock, I was still offended. I scowled for a while, and then realized that this was only adding to her amusement.

'You should have seen your face,' she cried. 'You look as if you were facing your greatest enemy. Eh, don't look like death, I was only joking.'

It was bad manners among our people to be angry with one's relatives. All of us—about five hundred or so—living in this cluster of homesteads came from the same ancestor, Odanta. So we were all cousins, or children of one great-great-grandfather. And even if you were allowed to be angry with your relative, it was not possible to be annoyed for long with your best friend. And especially if that best friend happened to be Ogoli.

I have never known another child in our Odanta who got into as much mischief as my cousin Ogoli. She would perform the most horrible acts and explain them away innocently, so much so that her listeners would believe in her innocence. She was thirteen, a year older than me. Her father, Obi Ibekwe, was one of the oldest chiefs in Ibusa, and he had many grown-up sons who worked their family farms, which meant they had more than they could eat in a year. And Ogoli, lucky girl, was the last born of her mother. And her mother was the senior wife of Obi Ibekwe. What more could a girl want!

I was not so lucky. My mother was the middle wife of Obi Okonitsha. So she had to do all the work in our father's big hut, and I was sent as a big gift from her personal god 'Chi' to help her. We had just enough food, because my father, though much younger than his kinsman Obi Ibekwe, was a good farmer. My mother got her one yam share every day. But the biggest and the best yams went to my father's senior wife.

Looking at Ogoli's face that afternoon, I decided that if I could not convince her that she had offended me, I might as well join in her laughter. So I started, reluctantly at first, then I found that my anger was melting away the more I laughed. I could see myself in my mind's eye, scratching my prickly back against a tree. I must have looked funny. In fact, I now wanted to prolong the fun, so I made an empty threat:

'You just watch out. I am going to pay you back in your own coin. I shall do the same to you one day, when you least expect it.'

'No chance, Ngbeke the daughter of Okonitsha. I am not a deep thinker as you are. You should have seen your face, like that of a baby being tickled!'

So I started to chase her and she ran round my mother's hut, until we both collapsed breathless, almost exactly where we started. One or two older people looked up at us perfunctorily and went on with their gossip.

'Do you know why I woke you up from your palm-tree sleep?' she asked in between breaths.

I shook my head: I did not know.

Then she blurted out, 'We can make twenty earthenware pots and ten lamps.'

'But how, and why?' I asked, perplexed at this really big idea.

'You'll see,' she went on darkly. 'We'll just have to be there in the banana grove and dig up a lot of good quality clay and then set to work. There is plenty of sun and it looks as if it's going to be just like this for many days to come, so they won't take long to dry.'

'But why?' I asked again. We modelled all manner of household utensils with clay. Our mothers sometimes made their own cooking pots, and dried them for days in the sun. The new utensils were then polished with old rags until they shone before being used for cooking. As this was regarded a very artistic work, women took much pride in displaying their pots and lamps. It would not be a bad idea to occupy ourselves with making such beautiful things on an afternoon like this one, which seemed so completely dead, hot, and exhausting. But why did we need to make as many as ten lamps and twenty pots, when my mother who was very good at it could only manage one or two at most in one afternoon?

4

Ogoli looked around us to make sure that there was nobody near. The two women across the path were too busy in their gossip to take any notice of us, and as for the young men having their hair trimmed next door to my mother's hut, we could be dead people for all they cared— so engrossed were they in making themselves handsome.

Then she came nearer to me still and touched the upper part of my arm. She was so close to me that the faint smell of akara balls she had eaten for her midday meal reached me. I did not mind this, for I was dying to know why we needed to embark on this great venture.

'You must promise me two things: first, that you will tell no one, and second, that you will work with me.' She moved away, looking at me sideways to see the effect of her announcement. Then she added in a whisper, 'It's a secret, see?'

My cousin was older, and was brought up to respect an older person. It was assumed in our town that the older someone was, the wiser the person would be. I used to doubt this belief many a time, especially when I thought about Ogoli. But if I doubted her wisdom, there was one thing neither I nor anyone else ever doubted about her, and that was her confidence. I think that confidence originated from her secure position in her father's big hut. (Her hair, for example, was always lovingly plaited by the younger wives of her grown-up brothers, and sometimes her mother, the senior wife of our whole village Odanta, would plait it for her! My mother was too busy looking after my father and his senior wife, to say nothing of my brothers and sister and myself to have any time in plaiting mine. That was why I always wore my hair cropped low, giving my head the look of a coconut that has lost its covering.) So despite the fact that Ogoli was not always in the right, she had a way of making me do what she wanted me to do. I kept hoping that one day I too would acquire this great gift of persuasion. But for the moment, I lacked the confidence.

5

'Are you going to promise to keep it a secret? It's a great secret,' she whispered again tantalizingly.

My heart started to pound in excitement. I nodded numbly, like a lizard resting in the shade. My nods were saying, 'I will do anything. I will help you make the pots and lamps, I will even keep the secret, if only you tell me all about it.'

'Then swear!'

I then touched the earth with my forefinger, licked it and pointed it to the sky, showing her that I had called upon those living in the earth and those living in the sky to be my witnesses. By licking the earth, I promised to keep my mouth shut.

My cousin was then satisfied. She came closer again, rubbing her back against the wall of my mother's hut. 'You must tell no one. You must ask no questions about it because it is still a very well-kept secret. If you ask me any question, I shall not tell you anything I hear my father discuss with the elders.' Then she paused dramatically, for a split second which to me seemed like ten years. She had been so much with the adults, she had watched them for so long, that she imitated their way of doing things, even the way they paused for dramatic effects in their conversations. Then she continued, 'We are having a new bride coming into our very cluster of homesteads in only a few days.'

'A bride! Our very own bride!' I whispered. My eyes grew round in wonder and excitement. A new bride meant eating and drinking and dancing for many days . . . and the preparations . . . our own new bride!

My cousin took up the lizard nodding now. 'Its true, its true,' she kept on saying in between nods, whilst I went on closing and opening my mouth and whispering: 'A new bride, a new bride.'

'And a new moonlight one,' Ogoli added for good measure.

But for the fact that I had promised to keep quiet, I

would have jumped at this last piece of news. I always liked moonlight brides, because there were so many secrecies attached to them. I had watched this celebration in other homesteads, but had never seen anyone arrive by moonlight in ours. Some of these moonlight brides had to be kidnapped because the elders suspected that they would not like the husbands chosen for them. But all we children knew was that we enjoyed the excitement of it all. A secret moonlight bride!

Thousands of questions formed themselves in my head, but as I had promised not to ask any question, I simply had to be satisfied with the little bit of information I had been lucky enough to get. I would have liked to know where the bride was coming from. And who among our men was going to be the new bridegroom. And why was she going to be a moonlight bride?

'We must start working on the gifts now, if they are to be ready in two Eke days' time,' she said, cutting into my thoughts.

'That will give us ten days,' I replied. Eke days were rest days on which people stayed away from the farms; on which women put on their best lappas and went to the market to sell their wares and buy things needed for their huts; Eke days were days when the latest dancers displayed their skills to the people of Ibusa. Eke days were days of celebration and days of joy.

But after a while reality started to set in. 'We will be in trouble though if we have to go into the bad bush and the banana grove to get the clay. You know we were warned never to go there again, and on Eke days like this when all the dead ghosts are said to be hiding in the bush, what do you think?'

'Ah, but you promised. You swore by the earth and by the sky. You said that you would help me. You promised to help mould gifts for our new bride. Think of all the praises we will get. That is why I have chosen to come and confide in you and not in our other cousins, Nwasiwe, Akeje, and the others. You know that they will all jump at the opportunity.'

That was true. The other girls were around the same age as Ogoli and myself. But we had been warned not to go to the banana grove because bad people were thrown in there after they were dead. And the place was a grove which snakes favoured on hot afternoons like this.

'If we are going, we might as well start right now. Your mother will soon call you to go to the stream with her or to help her in cooking the evening meal. I have not been to the market today. But if we start now, we'll be back in no time at all.'

'But the snakes, Ogoli, the ghosts!' I said weakly.

'Don't be a coward, Ngbeke the daughter of Okonitsha. Are you going or not? You promised. Think of the reward.'

'Yes, I will go.' I replied hurriedly, little knowing what it was that I was letting myself in for.

The Banana Grove

It was one thing to want to welcome our moonlight bride with new lamps and fresh earthenware pots, but to get the few tools we needed to make them was another thing. I had one more worry: how were we to keep the whole operation a secret from our parents, from our brothers and sisters, and from passers-by who would no doubt want to know what we were doing? But each time I opened my mouth to ask a question, I would look into my cousin's face and remember my promise. I just followed and did whatever she ordered me to do. I promised myself that never again would I make such a blind gesture to anybody. It was too late to go back on this one.

Despite my misgivings, I was equally excited by it all. Our first problem was how to get the sharp digging tools from our mothers' stacks of cooking things. I was to get the sharp, curved hand-knife my mother used for digging her cassava farm. As this was one of her most useful possessions, I knew I had to be extra careful. The trouble was that she kept it on the shelf in one of the rooms she liked staying in most. And on this afternoon, she was there sweeping up.

Ogoli had boasted that it would be easy for her to get her mother's wooden spike. This had a very sharp edge, almost like a sword. The younger wives in her family were fond of using this tool for digging up clay, when they felt too lazy to bend down for their work. It would be very useful to us because all we needed do was to put our weight on it, and down it would go. My mother's curved knife would then scoop out the clay.

I walked in quietly, so quietly that my mother looked up from her sweeping and asked, 'What's up, Ngbeke?'

'Nothing,' I said quickly in a small voice.

My eyes roamed the dark little room, and could make out the little shape of my baby sister, Awele, sleeping in the corner. I smiled a little as I noticed that she had kicked off the light lappa my mother had used in covering her.

'Don't wake her, whatever you do, because I still have a lot to do before we go to the stream,' Mother warned me.

'Oh no, oh no, I won't.' I knew that if she woke up now, I would have to look after her until her bed time. She was a nice plump three-year-old, but not welcome by my friends. I sometimes missed exciting games because I came out with my sister on my back. And I was sure that Ogoli would not welcome her in the banana grove this afternoon.

'Ngbeke's mother! Ngbeke's mother!' came a woman's voice from outside our hut.

'Who is calling me on a hot afternoon like this,' moaned my mother in an undertone.

I looked out quickly and saw that it was Nwasiwe's mother. She had probably finished gossiping with Ogugua's mother. So I told my mother who it was. 'And Mother, better go out and see what she wants, otherwise she will wake Awele, and we will have no peace,' I warned.

'You are right, daughter. But could you pack the dirt I have swept together.'

I was happy to oblige. This did not take me a minute. When I looked out of our hut, I saw exactly what I had expected to see. My mother had her back to the coconut tree, and was drinking in every word that came from Nwasiwe's mother's mouth. As for her, she was standing with feet planted apart and her arms akimbo, holding forth with all her energy.

And that was the break I needed. Quickly and noise-lessly so as not to wake my baby sister, I removed the digging knife from the rack and slipped out of my mother's hut, through the back doorway and into the little bush that demarcated our part of the village from those belonging to the Ogbolis. It was when I crouched in the bush that I started to wonder how Ogoli my cousin fared. Her own tool would be much more difficult to hide than mine. 'I just hope she manages to get it out all right,' I murmured.

I soon heard her giggling, pulling the spike behind her. 'I could not hold it upright you see, so I had to devise a way of dragging it along.'

'Well, we have made it, haven't we?' I asked reassuringly.

She nodded still giggling in excitement.

We decided to go the bush way so as not to be seen by anybody. So into the bush we plunged, on our way to the deeper forest beyond, in the banana grove. We soon came to the end of the bush, without seeing anybody. But when we neared the narrow track that divided the bush from the living area, we heard voices. We quickly hid behind the plantain trees that grew wildly along the track. I flattened myself against one of them and held my breath whilst two women and a man passed by. They were talking and arguing so loudly about someone who had duped another of some money that I was sure they would not have actually noticed us if they had looked at us. We knew all the three of them and had we been seen, it would have been necessary for us to greet each of them by their praise greetings. Because in our town, it was a mark of bad manners to pass another by without saying hello. And if you knew people's praise greetings, then you must use those as an extra mark of respect.

When they had gone, we started to emulate them and laugh at their gesticulations. How we laughed at their expense. Adult life was so full of trouble. They always had a great deal to talk about.

We soon entered the grove. It looked and felt as if we were entering into a darkened room. This was more so, after the intense heat of the day. We felt compelled to hush our laughter, as if told so by a hidden force. My feet seemed much heavier, and I started to have doubts as to whether we were doing the right thing. I thought I could sense Ogoli too had got cold feet. She did not say this aloud but I could tell from the way she was behaving.

The trees around the grove grew much closer here. So close were they that they shut off the sun completely. The fallen leaves were all moist and sometimes very slippery, even though it had not rained for many a day. As we passed slowly by, we could hear some frightened animals scurrying into safety. Some woodpeckers protested in anger, and a bush parrot started to jabber in a language best known only to himself. The sounds of these everyday animals seemed to have gained more in strength here. Everything took on an unearthly air—even the banana leaves seemed to have been elongated.

'I know,' announced Ogoli in a voice that had suddenly become strange in this strange place. 'If we answer these animals back—you know, make animal sounds—we will not be afraid, and they will think we are one of their kind.

I did not feel like answering her, so she went on jabbering like the wood parrots, then cooing like the wood pigeons. But the animals seemed to grow angrier than ever.

'Please stop, you are making it worse,' I screamed, putting my fingers into my ears.

Things did not improve when she started to sing our

age-group song. 'At least this will warn the really dangerous animals that we are coming.'

I knew what she meant by dangerous animals. They were the snakes, which I feared most of all animals. I also feared the ghosts of people thrown into this bush. I tried to join in the chorus of the song, but my mouth was dry, and Ogoli asked sharply, 'Ngbeke, you are not afraid of the wood parrots and wet leaves, are you?'

'Of course I'm not,' I snapped back, knowing that this was far from the truth. 'Only my mouth is very dry, and I wish I'd had a drink of water before we left.'

'Don't worry, we are there now, and nothing has eaten us yet.'

She was right, we were there, right in the deep banana grove. The sun had never reached this place, and the cluster of banana trees all seemed to have agreed to join at the top in a kind of eternal embrace. You could not tell for sure which wide green leaves belonged to which trees, and from one tree to the other. Creeping plants wound round from the ground to the trees, and from one tree to the other. We were surrounded by a riot of green. Moist green all over the ground, leafy green around us and on top of us. Flies and other tiny insects buzzed around and became even busier on our approach. So closed and humid was the place, that I felt for a time as if I were a prisoner in the belly of a thick, green bush: so damp, and sealed from the outside world.

'Let us get what we want quickly and move out. It is very ghostly,' I said.

'Yes,' replied my cousin. This time she neither argued nor laughed at me. She did not even hide her fear.

3

The Python

I stood there in the grove looking wildly about me in fear. Should I make a run for it and forget all about this bride whom I had not even seen yet, or should I start digging for the clay and try to forget our scary surroundings? For once, I did not look to Ogoli to tell what to do. She was too paralysed with fear to be able to think straight.

Then instinctively she started to emulate the adults. (When our parents were frightened of any scary presence, they would chase the thing and shout, 'Asha, asha' — meaning 'Go away, thing'.) Ogoli swung her spike in the air, shouting, 'Asha! Asha! Asha! If you are a ghost, we are not afraid of you. If you are an animal, we are not here to disturb you. We only come for some clay. Asha, asha.'

Her shouts and empty threats to the lurking animals took her mind off her fear and gave her back her lost confidence. But the effect on me was different, especially as the spike she swung in the air brought down damp cobwebs and rotten banana leaves. I was so shaken that a scream escaped my lips.

'Don't scream, let us hurry and go.' My cousin was back in command.

I cleared a small portion of the sodden ground with my mother's digging knife, and Ogoli began to clear the dirty first layer of mud away with her spike.

'I will have to do the digging because my knife is sharper and stronger than your wooden spike. We don't want to break the spike, that will put us in bigger trouble than we are already.'

'We are not in any trouble,' Ogoli said optimistically. 'But it wouldn't be right for you to do all the digging. I know. I'll sit here and count your digs. When it is a hundred, then I will take over and dig another hundred. Because you see, there are several layers of earth in this place covering the beautiful white, chalky mud. We don't want an inferior mud. You know what they say, good clay makes good pots, and good pots cook delicious food.'

We both laughed nervously at this. I noticed that this was the first laughter we'd had since we came into this sunless grove of green. But the animals did not even like our laughter. The wood parrots took up the sound of our laughter and started to repeat it over and over again, making the sleepy bats flap their tent-like wings about. So I said in a whisper, 'Just sit down there and count.'

She looked round and sat on the fallen trunk of a banana tree. She started to count in a singsong voice, marking the time with her spike. 'Ofu, abua, ato, ano . . . .' She counted very fast as I worked. Fear added to my speed, because I did not wish Ogoli to give enough time for the wood parrots to master the words. Racing against them thus became a great fun of its own. We smiled at each other, as we beat the parrots in their desire to copy the language of people.

But all of a sudden Ogoli jumped, colliding with me and shouting 'Nnam-e-e-e-e, Nnam-e-e-e-!'

I stopped digging, and all the flies and insects and wasps and other hidden creepy things, the names of which I did not know, that had settled down after our first disturbance, now burst again into activity. A cuckoo bird whose presence we had been quite unaware of burst into an angry monologue. 'Cuckoo, cuckoo, cuckoo, cuckoo,' it repeated, flying about us in anger. Ogoli, by calling her father in fear, had awakened some more sleeping bats, and one of them now flapped its wing just slightly above my face as if it was determined to give me a slap for interfering with its sleep. I too started to scream and call my father: 'Nnam-e-e-e, Nnam-e-e-e;' for what, I did not know.

I recovered first and asked, 'What was it that frightened you so, making you shake and call your father to help you?'

She did not answer, just stared at me, shaking as if she had been suddenly attacked by malaria.

'What was it that scared you?' I asked again, my fear coming back and my heart pounding in sympathy with Ogoli's feelings.

She pointed at the banana trunk she had been sitting on and said with quivering lips, 'Look, just look.'

I followed her glazed stare and looked at the trunk. I could not believe my eyes at first, for I thought it was the dark shadows playing us some tricks. But when I stared again, I knew then that there was no doubt about it. The seemingly dry banana trunk was no trunk at all, but a huge living snake that was having its nap, maybe after having a mouthful too much. Ogoli's cries and my screams were waking it up slowly, and right there, whilst we still stood screaming, it gave a mighty heave as if it was about to curl itself into a smaller heap.

Of course, we did not stop to see what it was going to do. We ran out of the grove. We forgot everything, almost everything, my mother's digging knife, Ogoli's spike. But funnily enough—I did not know how—I held on to a lump of clay in my hand. We screamed as we ran, falling over each other and tumbling into many rabbit holes, but we quickly scrambled up and ran on. Fear fuelled our speed.

We had forgotten that we had been told not to go into the grove in the first place. We had forgotten that our parents, especially our fathers, would be very angry with us for our disobedience. But so great was our fear that there was little time to think of our actions. All I did see in my mind's eye was a huge snake heaving itself up. Both of us were sure it would follow us and swallow us up for its next meal, as we tore ourselves from the damp bush through the footpath, in between the few passers-by, each of whom stared at us in wonder. One or two people tried to stop us and ask what the matter was, but gave up as they could not make any sense of what we were trying to say. We made little sense even to ourselves.

We soon reached the back of my mother's hut. We jumped over the herb-tea hedge and came to the front where a small knot of relatives stood, most of whom had been summoned there by our cries. They now faced us in anger, demanding to know why we had taken it upon ourselves to be screaming and behaving like children with no owners.

Afam, a male cousin of ours, who with his parents the Mordis lived in the hut next to my mother's, was a determined young man of eighteen. He had a strong sense of community spirit, and would do anything to protect the name of our small village Odanta. He now seized me by the shoulders and shook me so violently that my eyes wobbled. He said hoarsely, 'Stop screaming, girl. You are not born into a community of cowards. Stop screaming. What do you want our neighbours to say? Many people from other villages saw you shouting and tearing down the footpath. Stop it, girl.'

'And why did you go to the Ajofia, that frightening bush, on such an afternoon, when everybody is busy resting in the cool of their huts?' asked Nwasiwe's mother, her arms as usual akimbo.

'And making such a racket about it, as if the whole world

was falling down,' put in my brother Dike. I could see that he was ashamed of me. And they all were ashamed of Ogoli and me for behaving so badly, for what seemed no reason at all. The other part of the Ajofia belonged to the people of a neighbouring village, the Ogbolis. They must have heard us screaming.

I tried to explain to them that we went only because we were going to make pots and lamps to welcome our new bride. But I knew that my explanation would bring us into even deeper trouble, since we were not supposed to know anything about the new bride yet. It was still a bargain being arranged by the elders. So I kept opening my mouth and shutting it, like a fish on dry land struggling for air.

I looked round to see how my fellow sufferer Ogoli was getting on. My heart sank to find that she was suffering much more than I was. She had more to lose. Being an older girl, they expected her to know better. And instead of holding her head up, she let tears of humiliation and frustration wash down her whole face. She could hold her silence no longer. She told them all.

As I had expected, our people were horrified. I tried to tell Ogoli to stop talking, but once she had started telling them she felt compelled to go on. She tried to exonerate us by adding, 'But we meant no harm. We have not told anybody. We only wanted our new bride to feel welcome. We were going to keep it a secret.'

'Some secret!' snorted Afam the son of Mordi.

And everybody laughed at our expense.

'I don't know what the world is coming to. For a young girl to have the courage to go about repeating conversations she heard from men, senior men for that matter!' croaked an old woman who lived alone. Though this woman, Elege, was very bent in age and shrunken in appearance, she was respected for her openness and sincerity.

Everyone looked at her and nodded in agreement. 'Why

should Obi Ibekwe allow himself to lapse so by letting his youngest daughter hear what was being discussed in his compound?' I heard a group of women say in undertones. Obi Ibekwe was the oldest man in Odanta, so nobody dared question him openly. But he would soon hear of all this.

'Suppose, after this shameful episode, the bride's people now refuse to marry their daughter into this homestead, just because of your bubbly mouths?' asked Ogoli's mother, still in great anger.

As we had no answer to that question people started talking all at once, telling us what a bad thing our kind of curiosity was. Suppose we were unlucky enough to have come face to face with a ghost? they all asked.

Soon the waves of blames and counterblames subsided. Afam, as perceptive as ever, was looking at us rather closely. He suspected somehow that there was a reason for our fright. Looking me straight in the eye, he asked, 'So what was it that you saw? And what was it that put you in fright?'

'We saw a big snake, a big sleepy snake,' I said, glad to be given the chance to speak out at last. 'It's as big as a tree.'

'A snake as big as a tree?' Ogoli's mother asked in disbelief.

Then I saw my mother crying and at the same time pointing to the sky, asking God to be her witness, that she was doing all she could for me, and that if any evil should befall me, for doing what I was told not to do, it was my fault and nobody else's.

'But you don't need to cry, Mother, because it is true. I am not making it up,' I told her boldly.

'Did you see a ghost as well, a ghost as big as an elephant?' Dike put in. He had apparently come to the conclusion that Ogoli and I simply went hysterical for no reason at all.

19

'We did not see a ghost as big as an elephant or as small as an ant, but saw this large snake. It was very quiet and its colour was the same as its surroundings. That was why we did not at first know it was a snake. You go and see it, there in the grove,' I said in challenge.

Ogoli came to my aid and declared, 'I was sitting on it.'

This made them all stare at us again. We seemed to be coming up with such incredible statements—sitting on a snake!

'Are you sure these children have not seen a ghost or some evil spirit in that place? They seem to be talking nonsense to me,' said the old woman, making her point with her stick.

'But it is true,' I said, sticking my tongue up to the sky to show that I meant what I was saying.

Suddenly everybody went quiet. I stared at my feet, thinking that they had probably believed us at last. But when I looked up, I saw that they were quiet because the two Obis—Obi Ibekwe and my father Obi Okonitsha—were coming home from attending an important meeting in town. They were soon acquainted with our disgrace, and we were reprimanded in so strong a language that I personally would have preferred to have been beaten instead. Our mothers were told off as well, because the Obis were sure we were not told of the Ajofia, and the fault lay with our mothers. I considered this unfair, because Ogoli and I knew what we were doing. But no good child should argue with an Obi—a man with a title like our elders. So we all kept quiet, whilst they talked in their grave, wise voices.

They made as if they were about to go to their different courtyards, when I caught something like a conspiratorial look in their eyes. Then my father cleared his throat and asked, 'How long ago did you see this snake?'

'Just now, not long, Father,' I said happily, glad that at least somebody believed us.

'Well, Chima, Afam, you two get another young man with you and go and kill that snake. I think it is a python, that had just swallowed something big. If my guess is right, it will stay there helpless for some time still. Such a big snake as you have now described is too dangerous to live where people go for bananas and clay. It can swallow anything: goats, hens, even humans.'

'These girls did not realize how lucky they have been,' Ogoli's mother said, coming to our defence for the first time that afternoon.

'I sat on it, thinking it was a banana trunk,' Ogoli said, repeating herself for the benefit of her father, who had not heard that part of the story before.

'Good God, you were very brave!' Obi Ibekwe said dotingly. The fact that he loved and spoilt Ogoli was common knowledge.

'Brave,' snorted Chima. And everybody laughed.

'Well can you sit on a python?' my father asked him in joke.

'You should have seen them tearing down the footpath, as if the Devil himself was after them,' Dike declared.

The two Obis smiled knowingly, and my day was made. I knew that we had been forgiven. I even saw my timid mother smiling shyly and I knew that we would be allowed to make our pots and lamps for our new bride.

Four of the young men, who before had been busy cutting their hair, followed Afam and his age-mate Chima into the Ajofia to bring back the snake.

After they had gone a few paces my mother, now confident, called after them: 'Please be very careful, and don't forget to bring back my digging knife. It is the only one I have.'

'And my spike, and the clay we have already dug out,' Ogoli added.

And everybody laughed, as the young men of our homestead cluster put away their day-lappas and went into the bush in their khaki shorts, carrying clubs and axes, to rid us of the pig python that was living so near to our sleeping-huts.

4

Our Families

The two Obis walked away majestically behind their stool and staff-bearers. My father's staff-bearer was my older brother Udoji. His shaved head shone in the sunlight, and so did the armlet which he wore above his right elbow. His small loincloth, npe, had collected some mud patches, even though it was quite clean when he left home in the morning with father. One could understand why the staff-bearers' loincloths got dirty so quickly. They carried the staffs when the Obis were going out to a group dance or to places that would not involve sitting down. But the town meeting they had attended today involved sitting down, so Udoji had to carry father's public stool and not his staff. He was not allowed to sit on the stool himself, but would sit on the ground between father's legs. The meetings were held in open market places, and even though such places were swept thoroughly before the gatherings of the Obis, the red earth still clung to the npes of the bearers.

The Obis wore loincloths made of specially fine cotton.

Then atop of that, they had on another very big white cloth, homespun like npe, thrown over themselves, one edge going under one armpit and up to the other shoulder, toga-wise. This outer sheet, called otuogwu, was adorned with all sorts of patterns. My father's was spun by his senior wife, and it had patterns of pestles used in crushing yams in our odos, around the edges. Its whiteness dazzled in the sun, because my mother and I had washed it two days before, in readiness for this day of gathering of the chiefs in the big open market-place in the centre of our town, Ibusa.

My mother was very proud to be washing our father's otuogwu. She was proud also that her second son Udoji had been chosen to be father's staff-bearer, because father had seven other sons besides Udoji. Five of them were from his other wives. It was a great privilege to be a big man's staff-bearer because people say that such boys learnt the tricks of adulthood very early in life. They also learnt what was said in our town and saw the ways of the elders. My brother and Obi Ibekwe's staff-bearer simply stood in silence, listening to all the talk about Ogoli and me and the python. They did not even smile, so controlled were their emotions, the result of the long self-control they had to exercise at the gathering of the elders.

I knew as soon as our fathers had left that the little support we had from our other relatives would soon turn into jeers. As I did not wish to listen to the follies Ogoli and I made thrown back again at us, I quickly made my way to the back of my mother's hut. This place was a little hidden from the glare of my relatives and it had a long-lasting shade from the sun. My friend, cousin, and companion-in-disgrace soon sneaked away and joined me in my quiet sitting-place.

After a while, I said my thoughts aloud to her. 'Hey, Ogoli, did you notice that our fathers did not tell us off, or moan over us like our mothers?'

24

'Yes,' she agreed, and burst out laughing. 'Your mother was even crying—oh, she is so soft, your mother.'

'I don't think so,' I put in quickly in her defence. 'What can you do if you're a middle wife and your husband does not like you very much? You would expect your children to behave well at least, wouldn't you?'

I knew why she did not understand my mother's predicament. Her mother was the senior wife of an even bigger and older man than my father. So she was not used to women being apologetic about their position in their husband's house.

Luckily for my mother she had four of us. My two big brothers, myself, and my baby sister Awele. And my brother Udoji was my father's staff-bearer, so at least that was something. But I did not wish to brag much about it to my friend. She knew anyway.

'I am not bound by the promise I made earlier, am I, Ogoli?'

She shook her head. 'I broke mine too, didn't I. I told them all the news of the bride. Now they all know. So take a handful of earth and circle it around your head to show you that you are no longer bound by your promise.'

I wanted to point out to her that when she started telling our relatives about the coming bride, she did not perform any unswearing ceremony. But I thought better of it and did as she said, because I wanted to hear more about the bride. Having done that I asked impatiently: 'But why all these secrecies about our bride? A bride that will be here in two market days, and we still have to be quiet about it. Why?'

Ogoli started to giggle again. 'Maybe because our part of the bargain is very shaky.'

'What do you mean, shaky? Has the bridegroom no money to pay the bride-price? Who is the future husband anyway?'

Ogoli now laughed outright. She was so amused at her own thoughts that tears were running down her cheeks. I did not know what to make of her now. A short time ago her face was awash with tears of frustration; now what was I to make of her? So I let her be, though I was getting a little angry. I did so hate suspense, but I knew that if I showed any impatience Ogoli would hold the story from me longer. So, pretending not to be interested in whatever she was going to tell me, I looked with false intensity in front of us, at nothing in particular.

Then she gave me a playful nudge and said, 'You would be shocked if I told you that I did not know who the groom is going to be. As for the bride, your guess would be as good as mine.'

I stared at her in disbelief. 'You mean you raised all this rumpus for nothing? Oh, Ogoli, how could you?'

'I did not raise any rumpus. We both did, remember? The snake scared us, and we ran.' She looked serious for a while, as I opened and closed my mouth in wonder. How could Ogoli do a thing like this, I asked myself again and again.

'Well you did enjoy the publicity, the knowing looks of our fathers, didn't you?'

'Ogoli, is there going to be a bride at all, or is that a made-up story too?'

'You don't think I made that up, do you? I know a bride is coming to our Odanta homestead in ten days, but that is all I know. I guess I should have waited to know more before rushing to you. But from the secret way in which the conversation was being conducted, I suspected that it was going to be a moonlight one, and I was right. Our fathers would have corrected my story if I had told it wrongly. But I could tell that they were happy I did not know more. I think we will have to rely on the boys to tell us who the groom is going to be. They should know, because he is bound to be one of them.'

'Tell us? Not after our behaviour this afternoon, they won't.'

'You take things too seriously, Ngbeke the daughter of Obi Okonitsha. Why shouldn't your brother Udoji tell you who the bride and the groom are? He sits with the elders all the time. You should find out from him.'

I tried very hard to picture my serious-looking brother, Udoji, sitting down by our fireside and telling me all I wanted to know about the coming bride, but I failed. I would not even have the courage to ask him. That was one of the qualities expected of a big man's staff-carrier. He must be taciturn.

'Never mind, Ogoli, we shall all know in ten days.'

'You mean you can't find out from your brother? Then if I hear anything more, I won't tell you about it.'

I looked Ogoli again in the eye and burst out laughing. She asked why I was laughing at her and I told her she was the last person in this world to keep a secret like that. She saw the joke, and laughed too.

'In any case,' I said, 'it doesn't matter who the groom is going to be. We are determined to welcome the bride warmly with our lamps and cooking-pots, and that we shall do.' I said this more to convince myself that I still believed in all that Ogoli had been saying than for anything else.

We made a short trip to the pond in Ogboli just a few paces from the back of my mother's hut. We were able to get some muddy water with some broken calabashes. On our way back, my baby sister, now woken from sleep, saw me and waddled to me like a duck. She looked funny when she ran.

'Go to Mother, we are busy, go to her, do you hear me . . . go,' I said in mock seriousness.

She shook herself from side to side, standing there with determination. 'Take me with you, I want to play,' she whimpered.

27

'We are not playing, you fat duck,' laughed Ogoli. 'We are working.'

'Then I want to work with you.'

I knew my sister would not budge. If we made a big fuss, she would only howl and that would send my mother after me. I would then have to leave everything and take care of her. So in the end I stooped down and she jumped on to my back, piggy-back fashion. We soon arrived at the small enclosure we had chosen to work in. We only had a little clay but we knew that the young men who went to rid us of the python would not forget to bring our clay with them.

'I wonder how the young men are getting on with the python?' Ogoli remarked, as if reading my thoughts.

'I think they will be all right. There were four of them, to say nothing of those big clubs and cutlasses they were carrying. And Ogoli, do you think one of them is going to be the groom?'

My cousin's eyes lit up. She clapped her hands enthusiastically and said brightly, 'I think you are right, Ngbeke. But which of the four men would be the groom? I don't think they would have all gone so willingly to kill the python if none of them had anything to do with the coming bride.'

'But which of them? Chima has a girlfriend, she will be coming to her new home during the next yam festival. Afam has paid the bride-price for his, and the other two have regular girlfriends. They could not all have quarrelled with their brides-to-be?'

'You never know, do you? Anything can happen,' laughed Ogoli.

'Maybe he is the bridegroom?' I said, laughing and pointing to Chiyei, our village lazy man.

Ogoli was so overcome with amusement that she rolled on the mud ground. Chiyei was sometimes called our village idiot, but he was not really an idiot but a man who hated farm-work. He would not go to the farm, and when all the other men had gone to work he would just be walking round and round people's huts, wanting to be fed for free. If he ate in this hut today, he would eat in the next one tomorrow. This attitude of his was so well known that his praise-greeting was 'When will we come to eat in your house, Chiyei?' And he would shamelessly reply, 'When God provides.' We children usually ran away after saying this, because he could sometimes get nasty. But the adults would wait and say to him, 'God needs human, working hands to make his world go round.' Chiyei had never found any reply to those biting remarks.

And that was not all. They said that when he was young, his mother left him by the fireside during one bad Harmattan season. He was so deep in sleep that he rolled over and burnt his right foot. The foot had healed now, but he walked with an exaggerated limp; and the limp became more pronounced when he had downed kegs of palm wine. He was not only a great eater (he held the record as the greatest pounded yam eater in Ibusa), but he had a great capacity for palm wine as well. He had married several times before, but the wives ran away to their parents after a while. He had now apparently settled to living alone, because I had never seen him with a woman.

I looked up from the damp clay I was modelling and watched Chiyei as he made his way down the footpath in front of my mother's hut. It looked as if he was going to Obi Ibekwe's big compound. I started to giggle again.

'I would never marry a man like that,' I declared.

'Sh . . . sh . . . you must not say things like that. Suppose a man like Chiyei was chosen for you by your father, what would you do?'

I considered Ogoli's question for a while and shrugged my shoulders.

'You see, there is nothing you can do. You just have to accept the person chosen for you by your people. And look, Ngbeke, you must be loyal to the people of your clan.

29

Chiyei may be a lazy man, but we are not bad people. Our parents have told us many many times that a bride marries into a community, not just with her groom. Or would you want to marry the handome son of a witch?'

'Oh, no,' I answered very quickly. 'She would eat all my sons in the night, Olisa forbid.' I spat into the air to show how disagreeable this suggestion was. 'The way you are going on about Chiyei, anyone would have thought that he is the one getting a new bride.'

Ogoli had to laugh here. 'If he is the one getting a new bride, I am quite sure he would have shouted it from the roof-tops. No, I don't think he is the one. Maybe the new groom is your father?'

'What would my father want another woman for? No, Ogoli, I hope you are wrong. I am sure the groom is one of those in the bad bush, killing the python.'

My cousin nodded.

So assured, we sat down in the shade and set to work on our clay. We sang tunefully as we worked.

5

Wedding Preparation

'How are you geting on with the good work?' asked a voice from among the herb-tea bushes that formed a hedge around my mother's hut.

'Oh, very well,' Ogoli and I replied together.

Thus encouraged, our cousin Ogugua scrambled out of the tangle of the herb tea. We had thought we were well hidden. We had wanted the shapes and designs of our clay pots and lamps to be secret and had chosen this spot because it was partially hidden. But many people could hear our songs. Even Awele, my sister, joined in in her tuneless voice, but she would stop whenever we laughed at her. Then she would come and hide behind my back, sucking her thumb noisily. So we were not so surprised when Ogugua saw us.

'They are going to be very beautiful when they are finished. The lamps look like the dug-out canoes used for crossing the river into Onitsha.'

'You wait until we have painted them with uli leaves and put patterns on them. They will be the best lamps you have ever seen,' boasted Ogoli.

'I won't be surprised, because you are putting so much love and happiness into the work. . . . Please can I . . .' Ogugua started hesitantly.

I knew what she was going to ask. She wanted to join us but did not have the courage to say so outright, so she was praising our work first. I did not mind her joining but I was not quite sure of Ogoli, because it was originally her idea, not mine. But Ogoli was not going to make it easy for Ogugua. She pretended not to hear her. That cousin of mine, Ogoli, behaved so much like her father, the old Obi. I could see him treating people like that.

There was a little silence, punctuated only by Awele's finger-sucking.

'You won't mind my joining you. I don't mind if I have to do the fetching of muddy water from the pond. I know it was your idea, but I did not want to rob you of the glory. I only want to share it and to make the work lighter for you, and make our bride the more welcome.' It was a speech Ogugua had rehearsed whilst hiding among the bushes of herb tea.

In reply, Ogoli went philosophical. Success had many fathers, failure was an orphan. But since our parents did not blame us much for our disobedience that afternoon, the feeling of failure and humiliation did not last long. Was it not funny that the very people who condemned our boldness later admired it when they realized that if the python was left there, it would be a great danger to our livestock and even to us children? So they bathed us in glory. No, we would not stop Ogugua from sharing part of the glory. She could join and bring her own ideas and touches to the work: they would make the results even richer. So she welcomed our cousin, Ogugua.

'Nnua,' I said formally, as my respect for Ogoli went deeper. The serious atmosphere was immediately lightened by my baby sister who, like the bush parrots we saw earlier in the banana grove, copied everything I said. She too said 'nnua' to Ogugua, welcoming her to share our work.

We all laughed, and she quickly put her thumb into her mouth as if to seal it up. 'Now we are four,' Ogoli said in mock-seriousness.

'Awele is quite clever,' said Ogugua as she settled down on the earth, ready to join us in our work. Awele laughed, and bumped up and down on my back as if I were her horse.

Ogugua, being the newest in the group, was asked to fetch more muddy water. Without our saying anything about it, we all accepted Ogoli as the leader. I was in the middle, and Ogugua the new apprentice, so to speak.

We talked of many things, but the most important and burning topic was our new bride. We speculated many, many times on who she might be.

'Maybe she has a stump foot like our Chiyei,' Ogugua volunteered.

'And maybe her husband *is* our Chiyei. That will be stump foot marrying stump foot,' I said.

'Ngbeke! I am ashamed of you. What would your mother say, hearing you talk like that? Chiyei did not choose to have a bad foot, did he, it just happened,' said Ogoli, bringing us back to reality.

'I know what my mother would say. She would talk to Olisa as she did earlier about the Ajofia. And Olisa would listen to her prayers and turn me into a nice thoughtful girl. . . .'

There was no time for us to wallow in our speculation any longer, because we heard a loud noise coming from the forest. There were so many people rushing out of the banana grove. We stood up, temporarily forgetting our pots and lamps. I grabbed my little sister and she clung to me, ready to make a bolt for it. Then more people came out, and we saw that some of them were our young men who had gone into the Ajofia to kill the python. Four of them were carrying the huge snake. At first my mind could not focus, and I thought they were carrying a dead person who had been bitten by the snake. As they all came out into the open, I could see that no man could be that tall, not even a giant.

'It's the python, it's the python. It is dead. Our young men have killed it,' someone was shouting from among the jubilant crowd.

Everybody seemed to be running this way and that. I saw my otherwise cool brother Udoji dash out from our big compound and join the oncoming crowd. The carriers were smiling and, from where we stood as if transfixed, they looked very happy.

'Hey look, look at Afam. He is not looking too well. Has he been bitten by the snake, do you think?' Ogugua asked.

'Yes, she was right. Afam, the leader of the group, had lost his jauntiness and looked tired. His tiredness was more evident as he came nearer and we could see that his shorts and face had been covered with mud. There was only one way to find out what was happening and that was to go with the crowd. I put my baby sister on my back and followed, with Ogoli and Ogugua.

Many more young men who had gone back to making themselves handsome once more left their hair-cutting and joined the fast-forming crowd. It was such a noisy crowd, and the clamour of the voices could be heard as far as Ogboli. The carriers of the dead python were so moved by the crowd's shouts of surprise that they felt compelled to dance. They swayed the body of the dead python this way and that way, so that at first I thought they had managed to infuse life into the dead snake and that it was moving of its own accord. Of course it was all my imagination, based on the fact that I had seen the snake actually heave earlier on in the afternoon. As the excitement of the snake dancers increased, the snake assumed another form. It looked like the waves of the sea. But the dancers did not see all that, they were busy tossing the long, lifeless body of the python in all directions as they made their way to the courtyard belonging to Obi Ibekwe, the oldest man of our clan.

We, with the younger children and our mothers, followed the ecstatic snake dancers cautiously. There was a gap between us and them: we all seemed to be frightened of the mere presence of the python. My mother came nearer to me and touched my shoulder. She said with feeling: 'Do you know that a snake as big as that could have swallowed you and your friend up and still have had room for more?'

I shuddered in fear and then promised, 'I will never go to the Ajofia again on sunny afternoons.'

I was not the only person who was so afraid; Ogoli too seemed to have lost the power of speech. I moved nearer to her and touched her unfeeling arm with my free hand. She nodded at me and said, 'I know, we were very lucky. Mothers do not worry for nothing. We were so lucky.'

'I think so too,' I said.

Our mothers were very quiet, I could only guess their thoughts—that such a big monster could be lurking in our very banana grove which most of us visited almost daily in search of banana fibres for claying the floors of our huts. I wondered, though, what the python had been living on before this time.

We all trooped to the courtyard of Obi Ibekwe and we stood there waiting for him to come out from his inner room, where he had been resting after the long town gathering of the early morning. He was not a young man at all, in fact he was one of the oldest persons I have ever seen. I have always seen him as an old man; I could never imagine how he looked when he was young. He was so much older than my father, and I was made to understand that he knew many things. All the big happenings, the big quarrels and decisions were made in his courtyard.

His courtyard was built on a square, into which opened doors from the surrounding rooms. There was no ceiling in the square; instead there was a big opening through which came rain and sunlight. These courtyards were usually a big contrast to the surrounding sleeping-rooms: whilst the courtyards were open and bright and airy, the rooms were dark, airless, and close. But none the less, adults slept there.

There was a sudden hush as we all stood around the mud walls, watching the carriers of the snake. They still held on to it, and I wondered why this was so. But as I could not ask anybody, I simply stood there with my baby sister Awele still clinging to my back, watching everything.

Soon the youngest wife of Obi Ibekwe came out from one of the inner rooms carrying his snuff-pouch and pipe. She sat down on one of the mud seats next to the door of the main sleeping-place and started to fill the pipe for the Obi. Then noiselessly his staff-bearer came out from the same room and nodded to us all without saying a word. He too took his place by the door.

We then waited for what seemed an eternity, before people started to make way for my father as he came in. Wordlessly, like the others, he sat next to where the staff-bearer stood. Then he started to sing all by himself. He was suddenly transformed in my eyes, because he sang in words twisted and strange, pointing to the snake. I was so preoccupied with watching him that I did not notice when Obi Ibekwe came out from his inner room. Then my father made a pause in his solo. Obi Ibekwe went down slowly, his spidery legs scarcely able to carry his shrunken frame. He touched the snake with his horse-tail, and it was only then that the sweating bearers put down the dead python in the centre of the courtyard.

The older Obi signalled to his staff-bearer, who brought some chalk and three fat kola nuts. The two Obis then started to chant again to the snake. My father's low, steady voice and the older Obi's croaky one mingled together into what sounded like a kind of prayer, and also a thanksgiving. I could understand some of this latter chant because it was slower. But on the whole I still wondered how the

36

elders learnt all these various versions of our language and how they maintained the secrecy of it all, so much so that the meaning seemed to elude us, the ordinary people.

But this I could tell—that they were thanking the goddess of our river Oboshi for delivering Ogoli and myself from the jaws of this python; they were also appealing to the goddess to please send such pythons somewhere else because our clan was full of young children and livestock. All this was followed by a repetitive chorus which was gibberish to me, and I'm sure to many of us standing there, gazing at the toothless mouths of the two ancients.

After the chanting, Ogoli and I were called forward. We moved puppet-like, knowing little of what we were doing. My sister clung still to my back, like a crab on a cliff. She hid her face in the hollow at the middle of my back, after she had successfully rolled herself like a pumpkin.

The two men chanted over us as they drew the outline of the snake on our foreheads. They then broke the kola nuts into pieces and placed them all on a wooden tray brought in by Obi Ibekwe's youngest wife. The nuts were handed to Ogoli and myself first, before being passed round to the others. Throughout nobody spoke, and the only voices heard were those of the two Obis chanting their songs of prayers and thanksgiving.

It was then that the two Obis started to talk to each other and to the young men who had killed the snake.

'Do you think, big father, that the snake had been there long? I just wondered what it had been living on?' Afam asked, echoing my thoughts.

Obi Ibekwe cleared his ancient throat and shook his skull-like head this way and that way, whilst his deep-set eyes had a free run of us all. Then he answered. 'No, it had not been in our grove long,' he said gravely.

He would not go further, and Afam knew it was regarded as bad manners to pose many questions to one's elders. So he had to be satisfied with that basic answer.

All eyes were now directed towards Afam. He still looked dopey, like someone who has had a shock not too long ago. The Obi's glance at Afam was very penetrating, but he waited, demanding explanation without actually asking for it.

Afam felt obliged to clear his throat and to say, 'The python knocked me down, when I was too careless. I thought it was still asleep. But my friends here dragged me from under it. That is why I look so muddy.'

There were general 'ohs' and 'ahs' and everybody wanted to know how it actually happened. The other carriers did not wish to say much, so as to avoid embarrassing Afam. They all knew he hated anything melodramatic.

'I am all right. I am fine. No, the snake did not bite me. Please, I am all right,' Afam went on protesting amidst the shower of questions.

Obi Ibekwe raised his hand and we all kept quiet, rather unwillingly I thought, because personally I was convinced that our tall, wiry young man, Afam, was going to be the bridegroom. Why should he be so shy, if not for the fact that his bride was coming?

'Bring the esimesi drink, and let us thank our Olisa for the rescue of this young man.'

'Oh it is nothing, Father, I assure you. . . .' protested Afam, feeling very ill at ease.

More prayers were said as Obi Ibekwe poured some of the sweet-smelling, home-made gin on the mud floor. The bottle containing the drink was then handed round for all to take a sip. As this was going on, Obi Ibekwe said to my father in joke, but loud enough for all to hear:

'Our future in-laws would not regard us as a clan of cowards after today. I am glad about the python. First our daughters found it, then our sons killed it, and now I will leave it to the boys of this cluster of homesteads to do what they like with it, to prove to the rest of the people of Ibusa that we are not only brave, but artistic too.'

There was a hush, punctuated by the smacking of lips as the bottle of esimesi went round. We were all listening to what Obi Ibekwe was saying. I looked round and my eyes caught Ogoli's, and she nodded to me as if to say, 'Did I not tell you so, that there is definitely going to be a bride in our cluster of homesteads?'

'Oh Father, is there any umunna in this Ibusa doubting our bravery? Tell us who they are and we will show them. We will show them!' boasted my big half-brother Chima.

'Yes, who are they, Father?' Afam asked boldly.

'The mere thought of it! Was anyone doubting us?' asked Ogoli's mother, Obi Ibekwe's senior wife.

There was a murmur of discontent among our family crowd. If only the two elders would not be so secretive. What was wrong in having a new bride? Why should this one be such a hush-hush affair, almost robbing us of all the excitement?

'No, my children, it has not come to that,' said my father. 'You all know that a good wife is a wife of the community, it is only a bad woman who holds on tight to her husband and disregards his relatives. We need to prove that we deserve this new one who is coming.'

'The way you talk, anyone would have thought that she was as beautiful as the stars in heaven,' retorted his senior wife.

'Beauty is in the eyes of the beholder,' replied my father. 'This one would be as beautiful as the stars you talk about if her behaviour happened to be good.' The two Obis chuckled knowingly.

We were the more mystified. Apart from asking them point-blank who the bride was going to be and who was going to be the groom, there was no way of getting nearer to the truth.

The noises of sipping were still going on. Each of us would have a sip and pass the drink to the next person. Soon we heard the stump, stump of Chiyei. From the frequency of the sounds we knew that he was hurrying. He must have guessed that he was missing something. Chiyei loved drinks.

He smiled from ear to ear, and none of us could help laughing. I was glad of this interruption because the whole gathering was getting too tense for us all, what with the dead python on the floor and the two Obis telling us things we did not wish to hear.

'I heard about the python, at the stream, so I hurried. . . .' Chiyei began.

'You have not missed much, Chiyei. We still have another bottle of esimesi left,' said my father.

'Ah, but I have missed my share of the first one. . . .' Chiyei declared as his eyes followed the movement of the bottle. When it reached him, he almost snatched it from Chima. He put his lips round the rim of the bottle and had a very, very long pull at it. As we laughed, he took the bottle from his mouth to allow him to swallow his first pull. His amused and happy eyes seemed to be popping from their sockets. He laughed out loud, displaying his perfect teeth, and then to our surprise he closed his lips round the rim of the bottle again. This time, he kept swallowing the burning drink, just as if it were the spring water from our Atakpo stream.

'Hey, Hey!' shouted my father. 'Chiyei, Chiyei, the drink is for us all, not just for you! Just have a sip and pass it on, that's what you were told. . . . But you are finishing almost half the bottle all by yourself.'

Chiyei was now becoming dazed. He stood there undecided. He was debating with himself whether to finish the bottle and apologize afterwards. His face was working itself into different moulds and shapes like a lump of pounded yam being moulded in an odo. He puffed his cheeks until they looked like pumpkins, and glared, his watery eyes like those of an animal ready to pounce on its prey, and then looked again at the bottle.

40

We were all laughing whilst he struggled with himself. But my brother walked up to him, took the bottle from him gently, yet with a degree of firmness, and passed it round.

Chiyei gave in unwillingly. This surprised me a little, because I knew that he had got himself into a fight at slighter provocation. But his eyes still followed the progress of the bottle hungrily.

Then my father said something which puzzled us all. 'You don't want to start throwing your clothes about now, do you, Chiyei?'

'He enjoys doing that. So why is it so important that he should not do so now?' challenged his senior wife.

Only senior wives were privileged to question their husbands in a gathering like this. Women like my mother simply giggled and went on nursing their babies. My father ignored her, however, and she went on:

'There is one thing we do not lack in this umunna and that is an entertainer. We have the greatest palm-wine drinker here and also the greatest eater in the whole of Ibusa. Any bride should be proud to be married into an umunna like this one.'

'Yes, Father,' Ogoli said boldly, 'why don't we arrange to have a pounded-yam eating contest, then our Chiyei would win and it would be an added glory to us.'

People laughed and reminded her that Chiyei already held this title.

'No,' she persisted. 'I mean a contest between the whole of Ibusa and other towns so that people would pay to come and watch the eaters. . . .'

'And that will make our Chiyei a rich man. Well, well, well, we will remember that when we go for the final bargaining for the bride.'

'I wish we knew who she is,' Ogoli said in a small voice.

We all had to laugh again, because she had spoken for all.

'How can we tell you who she is,' said my father, 'when

we don't know if she would accept a member of our umunna as her husband? But her name is bringing us luck already. So I would suggest you young men treat the python well, flay the skin as artistically as you can. Remember to preserve the oil, it is very good for curing convulsions in babies. But for this bride, we would not have known of this big python. I think it is a good sign.'

We all started moving away, but Chiyei rushed for the empty esimesi bottles and started to lick them noisily.

'Let me pass,' Chima said. 'There is no more home-made gin in those bottles, they are empty now. Maybe it's because of people like you that brides don't want to come here any more. You have never done anything to boost the name of this umunna.'

'That is not true. I made our umunna famous. You go into the town and ask them where Odanta is and they will say to you that Odanta is where Chiyei, the greatest eater on earth, comes from. Some brides will even want to marry into this community because of me,' he said boastfully, sticking his large chest out.

'Yeah, you will be telling us that some girls would even want to marry you,' Chima went on.

'I don't see why not. A man is never ugly in Ibusa. And I'm not going to be the first ugly man created,' Chiyei said as he limped his way to his hut, licking the empty bottles.

'Did you hear that?' my mother asked Ogugua's mother.

'Are they getting the new bride for him then?' Ogugua's mother asked.

'Honestly, I don't know. Maybe she is coming to our Obi.'

'Oh, no!' laughed both women. They would have said more but they saw me looking at them.

'Go and play with your friends, Ngbeke, and stop listening to adults' talk,' laughed my mother.

6

Ogoli's Pride

Life went on almost as normal for the next few days. But you couldn't fail to note the ripple of excitement that affected all of us. The young men of our village worked hard on the python they had killed. It was another Eke day, and the next one would be the day our bride would arrive. We heard those who had been permitted to see the python skin say that it was the biggest one they had ever seen; the young men would not allow us into their bachelor hut to have a look. But I could tell they were busy, from the nice smell of the snake-oil that escaped from their door.

After the midday meal, Ogoli, myself, and Ogugua went to our own secret place too. If the young men were not going to show us how far they had gone with their flaying, we too were not going to let them see how we were getting on with our lamps and pots. We felt cheated, though, because we had found the snake.

'And do you know,' Ogoli informed us, 'somebody from Akulasi is going to buy the flesh of the python? I don't know how much he's going to pay for it, but I know they are using the money to cook the communal meal for the day.'

'I didn't know that people ate snakes! Ugh! I can't even touch it, even though it's dead,' said Ogugua, making her face ugly.

'As for me, I keep remembering seeing it heave, even in my sleep,' I said.

'I know,' said Ogoli, 'I can never forget the feel of that snake on my bottom as long as I live. It simply heaved me up. I didn't know what to think.'

'Well, since we can't eat the meat, why not sell it?' I said quickly, as I did not wish to be reminded of the terrifying happenings in the Ajofia on the last Eke day.

'If these lamps are going to be used for the next market day, we simply must finish the moulding and shaping today,' said Ogugua.

'I know,' I said. 'But what worries me is the drying. If we're going to decorate them as well, we must make sure that they're completely dry, otherwise the uli dye will run into the wet clay. So we need to sun them for at least three days.'

Ogugua picked up one of the finished but still damp lamps and started to admire it, holding it to the light. 'Oh, we don't have to worry about drying them in the sun. The shed over our cooking-places would do quite well.'

'That is a very brilliant idea,' Ogoli replied.

Ogugua was jubilant, happy that her idea was being considered and adopted at all by Ogoli and myself. She was well aware that we were doing her a favour, because the idea of making clay utensils for our coming bride was our own brain-child.

'So when we finish shaping them,' I said rather excitedly, 'we will take them a few at a time to the mud shed on top of our fireplaces. And before morning they will dry hard and shiny. On our way to the Atakpo stream we'll gather enough uli leaves to pattern the lamps.'

But I was soon cut to size.

'My mother's shed is full of dry meat, which Father brought from the town's public gathering yesterday,' Ogoli said with undisguised pride. 'So we have no space at all for drying mud lamps in our huts.'

By saying that, she had put Ogugua and myself in our proper places. Ogugua's father was not a red-cap chief. He was therefore not qualified to have shares of meat from public sacrifices, or public fines, as Ogoli's father and sometimes my father could. Among our people, offenders paid their fines with goats and chickens. These were usually killed by the town's butchers and the meat shared among the Obis. The older an Obi was, the more share he would get. So in Ogoli's family, there was always a large supply of eating-meat, because not only was her father an Obi, he was very old as well—one of the oldest in the whole of Ibusa. My father was an Obi too, but much younger, and he had not been an Obi for long, so he was not so illustrious.

We swallowed Ogoli's insult and said nothing for a while. Such times when she said things like this, I almost hated her. But we were taught that hatred was a bad thing, especially the kind of hatred you harbour in your heart; they said it poisoned the blood. One must either forget to hate, or have the hatred brought to the surface by having an open fight with the person who had offended you. And then after the fight people would judge and put the blame on the offender, and you two would share a piece of kola nut and make it up.

But on this afternoon there was no time for fighting and making up, so I decided to forget Ogoli's arrogance. Ogugua decided to do the same too. For she broke the uneasy silence and said, 'We have a lot of drying-places on our apata. And my mother would not mind at all.'

I gave her an encouraging nod. Ogoli looked away, pretending not to see us.

'Ngbeke! Ngbeke oooooo! Ngbeke eeeeeee!'

I knew that it would be too much to expect—my having a whole free Eke day to play with my friends. My mother would be needing me. I was sure she needed me urgently as I could tell from the way she drew out every syllable of my name.

'I wonder what the matter is now. We'll never finish these lamps now,' moaned Ogoli, echoing our thoughts.

I was wondering what the matter was too, for it was not time yet for cooking the evening meal, neither was it time to go to the Eke market which started towards sundown. So what was my mother calling me for?

'There's some consolation though,' I said, venturing to pacify my disappointed friends. 'We've finished all ten lamps. . . . I think the lamps are the most important items, because we'll need to carry them to welcome our bride, won't we?'

'Yes, we know that!' retorted Ogoli. 'You can claim that the lamps are not important too, just because your mother wants you to come and clean her nose for her.'

'I have never seen a bride arriving at her husband's house without his people carrying oil-lamps to welcome her, moon or no moon. Many times the moon didn't appear when expected, and so the young lamp-carriers would light her to her new home. I'm not saying the twenty pots are not important, but all I'm saying is that if we are very short of time, as the bride is expected on the next Eke day, we will have to make do with the lamps we have already finished. And Ogoli, you are getting very insulting these days, and I don't think I like it.' I finished almost breathless at my outburst. I was surprised at my courage.

Ogugua as usual nodded in agreement: her attitude seemed to imply, yes, Ogoli was getting too swollen-headed. And if she thought that because her mother was a senior wife and her father an old red-capped chief she was going to rule the whole world, then she was not going to rule us!

Aloud Ogugua said, 'If you can't come back and join us, Ngbeke, I shall take the finished lamps to my mother's mud shed, and when we go to the stream tomorrow we'll get the uli colouring leaves.'

'I was only joking,' Ogoli said, contrite. 'I didn't expect you to go and wipe your mother's nose. The trouble with you two is that you don't listen to adults' conversations to know that they say things to each other without meaning any harm at all. I listen to them many, many times and I know. Why should I pick quarrels with my best friends and relatives, relatives who are like sisters to me? Tell me, can a tree make a forest? My father always asks that question and nobody has answered him yet. You can't answer it either. I am only concerned in case we are unable to finish the whole thing before the arrival of our bride, next Eke market day. Please don't take it too badly.'

I must confess that pride fitted Ogoli much more than humility. When she went humble and near tears as she was now, she had a way of making those who had reduced her to that level feel guilty. She had done it again now. And Ogugua and I looked at each other sheepishly as if we were in the wrong in the first place. I didn't know what to do or say next.

But Ogugua was determined to press home her advantage. Maybe she felt that we had kept her down for so long, just because she joined our group much later. 'Twenty pots are rather too ambitious, don't you think? If we spend the next two evenings beautifying these ten lamps, people would say we've done well.'

I felt like running to Ogugua and hugging her. I had felt like that about the pots all along. After all, any bride, however poor her people, would come to her new home with enough over-decorated pots to last her for a long while. And whatever we made would be a poor show compared to those specially moulded by experts in pot-making. I didn't wish to offend Ogoli, and had gone on in the hope that somewhere along the line she would realize the folly of such an unattainable ambition. Now Ogugua had said it.

Judging from the look on Ogoli's face, it seemed as if she had been waiting for someone to tell her this. For since the night of the python we had worked four whole evenings, just to get the lamps ready. And we only had four more nights before the arrival of the bride. All we had time for was to dry the lamps on cooking-sheds overnight and polish them the next day in readiness for the patterns and designs we intended putting on them.

'We'll have a whole day just putting designs on the lamps,' I said. 'What fun we are going to have!'

'Oh yes, what fun! So we can relax now and make improvements on what we have produced so far. That will be better than preparing fifty utensils, and none of them a beauty,' said Ogugua finalizing her argument.

We waited expectantly for Ogoli to say something. But she took her time to come round to our way of thinking. She made another point though, which was a bit worrying, for she pointed out that the young men were taking the greater part of the glory. They were flaying the python, selling the snake-meat, and keeping the oil from the snake for medicinal purposes. And they didn't make much noise about it. In fact, they kept theirs a secret. And we who had made so much noise about ours, yelling all the way from the Ajofia to Odanta, could produce only ten lamps. But Ogugua countered her argument by asking:

'Who saw the snake first?'

'We did!' we both shouted in reply.

'So,' I said, 'next to the bride, we will still be the centre of the show. If we hadn't found the snake there would be no python skin, no oil, no money for the communal meal.'

Then my mother came out of her hut and shrilled, 'Are you deaf now, Ngbeke? Did you not hear me calling you all this time? Get up from that clay, we are going to the

Atakpo stream to fetch water, before the start of the market. So hurry.'

I smiled at my friends and we knew that even if we had all agreed to make twenty pots in addition to the lamps we had already made, time would be against us. Because being girls, we were all expected to help in the housework. The boys were not expected to do this, so they could spend as much time as they liked in flaying the python.

I left them to take care of the lamps so that I could follow my mother to the stream.

7

The Groom

My mother and myself got ready our water-gourds in front of our huts. Then she said to me, 'Ngbeke, go to the big hut and get some of your father's dirty work-clothes for us to wash. Just get the small ones, don't get any otuogwu, because we are not staying long at the stream.'

'You don't want me to bring any of my brothers?'

'No, Ngbeke. Don't go nosing into their bachelor hut. They are busy with some secret about this coming bride. Have you seen any of them since the midday meal?'

I shook my head. Now that my mother mentioned it, I noticed that the whole footpath was quiet. There were not even any young men in the barber's shed in front of Mordi's hut, trimming their hair as they were accustomed to do. 'Where could they have gone?' I asked my mother aloud.

'I don't know.'

I ran down the footpath to my father's hut, and picked up the few little things that needed washing. I could not help peeping into my big brother Chima's hut on my way back. But all I was able to find out was that the smell of the burning snake was very strong. I was too scared to go inside, because I knew that my half-brother Chima would not like it. They were always having meetings and discussing things in low tones, those young men of ours. But on this afternoon, I knew that there was nobody in the hut. Not wanting to be face to face with a dangling snakeskin, I skipped back to my mother.

I noticed that my mother had not been to Ogugua's mother's hut to buy the cake of blue for the washing we were going to do, and as I opened my mouth to say so, I saw that my sister Awele was clinging to her. 'She wants to go to the stream with us,' my mother mouthed to me over her head. I laughed at this, because it would take us ages if she were to go with us. So I had to go to Ogugua's mother's hut to get the blue, whilst my mother took Awele round our cluster of homesteads to find out who would look after her for us whilst we were away.

'I see you are going to the stream. Is your mother going with you?' Ogugua's mother asked after I had paid for the blue. She was a widow and sold blue to make ends meet. Her hunter husband died a long time ago, when my friend Ogugua was only a baby.

'Yes, she is going, but we shan't be staying too long . . . just to wash a few things and bring back some drinking-water.'

My last statement made her laugh, displaying her broken and uneven teeth and making her fat face puff like a mango. 'Have you ever heard of anybody go to the stream and not bring back any water?'

'Yes, I have,' I said quickly. 'My brothers do sometimes. They would just go to the stream, swim, then catch a fish or two and then come back empty-handed.'

Ogugua's mother laughed louder still. 'You're very young, Ngbeke, the daughter of Okonitsha. You forget that your brothers are boys. And that boys will always be boys, but girls become mothers.'

'Look, they have all disappeared this afternoon to God knows where. And that's my mother over there looking for someone to look after Awele for her. . . .'

Ogugua heard my voice and rushed out from their inner room, where I knew she had been busy stacking our lamps as her mother stood outside picking her teeth.

'Mother, I am going to the Atakpo too, with Ngbeke, Ogoli, and the others.' As she said this she placed her water-gourd on top of a tray, and started to rub some oily soap on top of her close-cropped hair.

Her mother looked at both of us, smiled again, and said, 'I think I'd better come along too, since I'm doing nothing till sundown.'

By the time we eventually set off for the Atakpo, we had quite a crowd of people: my mother and her friends, and about ten of us children. It was always like that in our cluster of homesteads in Odanta. When you wished to go to the farm and you let it slip and told one person, everybody who had been thinking of going but was unable to make up their minds for one reason or the other would say to you, 'But can I come too?' This was so much part of our everyday life that any loner was regarded as almost a mad person. You could never be a loner in our village. You were never allowed to, because our people said that a single palm fruit could never make oil, but when it was pressed with the other palm fruits, oil would be produced in large quantities.

We progressed noisily to the Atakpo stream. There were gourds rattling against each other, while some little children were given tins for their water, because little girls broke many gourds on their way back from the stream. The stream was such a long distance from home that any tiny drop of clean water was worth bringing home. Tiny girls were thus encouraged to contribute their energy to the housework, however little the contribution.

The adults, our mothers, were walking in front, talking

about their various businesses. I didn't know why this was always so. Whenever we were going to the stream, to the market, to anywhere, we children were always lagging behind. We only walked up to the adults when they called us or when the particular conversation they were holding was of special interest to us. Otherwise we let them go their own ways and we went ours, coming right behind them.

As we turned the corner, around the C.M.S. church, we impulsively started to run. We ran so fast that we forgot our little sisters who screamed after us, begging us to wait for them; we tore past our gossiping mothers, in our eagerness to be at the udala tree. It was always a case of first come, first served. But on this afternoon, even though we rushed into the bush surrounding the tree, there were no fallen fruits. We walked round it several times, our footfalls crumbling the brown dry leaves. There were one or two damaged fruits, their tempting juicy flesh open for all to see, but we felt reluctant to eat those.

But when we looked up, our mouths started to water like those of hungry dogs. For on the top of the tree were ripe, fat, fleshy udala fruits. In my own imagination I thought the ripe fruits were beckoning us to pick them. We eyed each other surreptitiously for a while, knowing what we would have done but for the fact that our mothers were not too far away. We would have climbed the tree. But our mothers would tell us that climbing trees was only for the boys, so we started to walk round and round the big tree singing:

> Udala fall on me, fall on me.
> I am an orphan and have had no food,
> Udala fall on me, fall on me.

We all joined in the song, skipping round and round the tree, begging the ripe fruits to fall on us. Our mothers walked up to us, then passed us without looking back. They knew we would catch up with them, by and by. And I was sure that they thought that we were only going to sing round the tree. But they were wrong. We were waiting for them to turn the corner away from the main road to the bush path leading to the stream.

Ogoli said: 'I shall climb that branch and shake it. You all do the collecting.'

'But our mothers will know because we will have so many fruits,' pointed out Akeje, one of the girls who was going to the stream with us.

Ogoli gave the girl such a pitying look. A look which said 'I'm sorry for you, you coward.'

We all laughed at this, because Ogoli's look was so eloquent. The girl felt so small that for a moment I thought she was shrinking before our eyes. I felt so sorry for her that I thought I would take it upon myself to explain why Ogoli was taking that attitude. 'Do you know that if Ogoli and I had been frightened, we wouldn't have found the python? And when a big python like that is hungry, it would come inside the huts.'

'I even sat upon it!' boasted Ogoli again.

Akeje's eyes opened wider. She had apparently not heard this side of the story. And she wanted to hear more, but we could not wait to tell her the details because we had to hurry. Ogoli made for the tree, ready to scramble up it, when I shouted to her: 'Stop, Ogoli, stop! Look, our mothers aren't turning into the bush path. They've stopped walking. Look, something is happening over there.'

Yes, something was happening. We could hear the wailing voices of our mothers, some of them were beating their breasts and shouting and pointing at something coming up the bush path.

'Maybe it's another python,' I gasped.

We forgot our udala tree, and ran down the road. The little girls were now crying in horror. Soon we saw a frightening procession coming from the bush path.

Our young men were coming from the path carrying what looked like a dead body. This time it was not a snake but a person, lying on the stretcher with only a loincloth on. We soon caught up with our mothers, and joined their crying. We didn't know who was so mummified with mud and loincloth, but the person lay so still and looked very dead.

'Who has met with such a bad accident?' Ogoli's mother asked.

'It's Chiyei. They almost killed him. He'll be lucky to be alive, just because—just because he has been led to ask for their daughter in marriage,' explained Chima in a grave voice.

'Chiyei! Chiyei! So Chiyei is the groom?' I asked Ogoli in wonder.

Ogoli covered her mouth, too stunned to say a word. We saw marks of beating on Chiyei's dark and mud-caked body.

I could see that our mothers could have laughed at this unusual announcement but for the seriousness of the circumstances. They were all trying very hard to keep a straight face.

But Ogoli's mother, being the eldest person present, said authoritatively: 'Take him home. I have never heard such a thing in my life. Since when have men been beaten just because they wish to marry a bride? I know she is a nice girl but Chiyei does not deserve this kind of treatment.'

We had by now crowded round her, drinking in every single word that came from her mouth. The shock of all these revelations was incredible. The boys saw Ogoli's face, and my younger brother Dike started to laugh.

It was like a spell breaking, that laughter. We couldn't help it any more. And to cap it all, Chiyei started to move on the stretcher. 'That's my luck, just my luck, I have to be beaten just before I marry a woman.'

'Take him home. We will soon join you.' Ogoli's mother's voice cut in like a sharp knife.

'How come they all went to Ude on Eke's day?' my mother asked as we watched the sad procession trailing back, with their load of Akayan roofing leaves, and the big body of Chiyei stretched on the bamboo sticks caked in mud.

'You all run along to the stream, come on, run along,' commanded Ogoli's mother.

We dared not disobey her, being the wife of such an important person as Obi Ibekwe, and his senior wife too. I knew she would give a reply to my mother's question, but she wanted to make sure we were out of hearing.

With Ogoli leading, we sped past our mothers, whooping with joy and expectation, as our excitement rose with this mysterious new bride.

8

At the Stream

The bush track through which we ran was not a straight
one. It meandered this way and that, here covering us up,
and there exposing us. We soon came to a point at which
we were well covered up from our mothers by a thick
growth of green bush, not too far from the stream. Ogoli
stopped running and flopped heavily on to some dry twigs
near the track. She was out of breath, as were all of us. I sat
next to her, and lowered my water-gourd gently in between
my outstretched legs.

'This is the biggest surprise of all: that our Chiyei is the
groom!'

'I know,' I said, 'but will they let him marry her – her
brothers seem to be against it.'

'Maybe because she is too beautiful,' said Ogugua. 'I
wish I knew who she is.'

'Anybody is more beautiful than our Chiyei, we all know
that,' I said.

'No, we don't,' Ogoli came in sharply. 'Ngbeke, I don't
know why you say things like that. Chiyei is from our

umunna, you know. Can't you see that we have been insulted—can't you? Even if she's as beautiful as Mammy Waata from the sea, her people have no right to treat our Chiyei like this. Don't you know it is not permitted to say that a man is ugly? The words ugliness and old age apply only to women, not to men.'

'Don't men get old then?' Ogugua asked in a noncommittal voice.

'No, they don't. Men mature, women age. A man is not expected to be beautiful or ugly. He is expected to be strong . . . you know, to be a man.'

We all kept quiet, remembering that her mother had said something like that earlier on. But nobody was bold enough to tell her so. Ogoli always copied what the adults said.

'I can't wait to get home from the stream. It's so exciting,' Ogugua said abruptly.

'Me too.'

We got up and ran down the muddy side of the stream. It was like entering a hole. You heard voices of people and the noises of the stream coming to you from below and for a while you saw nothing, except the thick walls of green pressing at you on both sides.

We ran down this seemingly muddy hole and soon came to the level of the stream. There were fewer people today, as it was Eke day and many families would have visited the stream and done their bits of washing in the morning, so as to leave the afternoon free for the big market.

We became the centre of attention. People stared at us. They had all seen our group of young men pass the stream on their way home, carrying Chiyei. There was no doubt, they had all been talking about it.

One woman looked up from the cassava she was washing and asked no one in particular: 'Have you seen your kinsman Chiyei beaten up? If I were Chiyei, I would never marry a girl who allowed her people to treat me like dirt.'

58

'Well you are not Chiyei, so shut up,' said Ogoli in a low tone.

We burst out laughing, and the woman demanded to know why. Nobody said anything. Luckily, before she could become a real nuisance, our mothers could be seen coming down the slope. They took in the situation at once, and so hurried us up. We guessed then that the whole of Ibusa would be talking about our umunna for a while.

As the stream was not so muddy, because there were not many people, I thought it would not matter so much where I got our drinking-water from. I picked up our water-gourds and started to fill them with water a few paces from where Ogugua and I had just had our bath. I was fully occupied with this task when my mother's voice reached me, loud and harsh.

'You do no such thing, you lazy good-for-nothing girl. Who wants to take home muddy water, eh? You tell me. We've walked over two miles to fetch drinking-water and you can't walk two paces to the clear area for some nice clean water.'

'But you told us to hurry, because of Chiyei and his bride. . . .' I began lamely.

Everybody at the stream was laughing at me now. It was a silly excuse, I knew, but we were all so impatient to get home.

'You mean you have to drink muddy water today because your kinsman Chiyei was beaten up for his bride?' said the curious woman who had just been asking us about Chiyei. There was sarcasm in her tone. Our mothers rightly ignored her, but I felt very small, and that took away my excitement a little. The other girls learnt from my mistake and took the trouble to wade openly to the clear inner area for their water. They all got praise from their mothers.

I sulked all the way home. And the big job of walking

back home from the stream did not improve my mood. On our way back we had to walk against the incline; it was just like climbing a steep mountain, where the only help you got came from the steps made by the feet of generations and generations of our people. Thousands and thousands of them must have climbed this slope, thousands and thousands of them must have washed in this stream, must have fetched cooking and drinking-water, just as I was doing now with my friends. But on this day I lagged behind, not just because of the steep incline, but because I was still nursing my hurt from my mother's telling-off. So I kept closer to our mothers than to my friends. I was not in a mood to take part in my friends' chatter.

Then I heard Ogoli's mother say: 'I hope we succeed in getting Chiyei settled down this time, once and for all.'

'I hope so too,' replied Ogugua's mother. 'But her brothers have acted so badly.'

'I know,' said my mother. 'Our Chiyei is not the best man in Ibusa, but he has a kind heart. All he needs is a good woman to hold him together. This girl should be good for him.'

'Well, I don't know if the bargaining would go through now,' said Ogoli's mother. 'Do you know that it was Chiyei who organized our boys to go to the akayan farm with him this afternoon, to get the roofing leaves for his would-be in-laws—just to prove that he could work harder if he wanted to.'

'Well, our cluster of homesteads can use those akayan roofing leaves,' began Ogugua's mother. 'My hut is full of holes, I can tell you.'

The other women laughed at this and said to her: 'But you are not being wooed now. You belong to the umunna, nobody is trying to impress you into marrying into Odanta.'

'Chiyei is trying to impress his wife-to-be. His very, very fair wife-to-be,' Ogoli's mother finalized.

My mother turned round at this point and saw me

walking closely behind them. 'Just look at that sneaky daughter of Okonitsha. She's been listening to all we have been saying.'

The other women simply laughed and Ogoli's mother said: 'We have not been saying anything which she did not know already.' She turned round to me and asked: 'Why are you not with your friends anyway? They did not tell you off, your mother did. And, young daughter—a girl, a good one is not expected to sulk for so long. Go along and walk with your friends.'

Ogoli and the others could not believe their ears when I told them that it was Chiyei who had arranged for the visit to the akayan farm in Ude.

'He must have felt awful when the python arrived and people were laughing at him for not working hard,' Ogugua observed with sympathy.

'I know,' I said. 'I think that incident spurred him into action. I don't care who she is now, but I'm proud that our Chiyei really tried his best.'

'A lucky bride, I must say. First she's having the python skin, all well prepared for her, then her would-be husband has organized akayan to be supplied to all the members of her family, and our ten beautiful lamps . . . I have never heard of a bride more welcome than this one.'

'She didn't know all these secret preparations, though,' said Ogoli.

'Well, I think that's what our men and boys should be doing. Telling everybody what a nice and welcoming umunna we are, not just a passive one that will take the beating of one of our men lying down and doing nothing about it,' Ogugua said with heat.

'Maybe they are doing something now,' suggested Ogoli. 'You never know. After all, today is Eke day, and everybody is at home. If they are going to act, today is the day.'

Anger fuelled our determination and we walked fast, past our mothers to our cluster of homesteads. What we were really going to do to those who had hurt our kinsman Chiyei was not quite clear, but we were going to do something!

9

Sensible Bride

Our shadows were lengthening by the time we walked into our umunna. It was nearly the time for the evening Eke market. Whilst anger still burnt inside us, we were expecting our cluster of homesteads to be full of activities. But apart from a few goats chewing the peels of yams thoughtfully, all was silent. Even the front of Mordi's house, where everyone met to gossip and to have a haircut, was quiet. The benches and chairs were there, but not a single person.

'Have they all left this umunna then?' Ogoli asked with a giggle.

We all laughed nervously as we made our way down to the end of the footpath, which ended with Obi Ibekwe's large compound. Ogugua branched into her mother's hut, but I had to walk further because the drinking-water I was carrying was for my father. Ogoli was going to her home at the end of the path. Then we were stopped by our men, rushing out of Obi Ibekwe's big central hut.

'The greatest shame of it is that we have never treated anyone like this before. We don't want her any more,'

Mordi shouted with heat as he walked out of Obi Ibekwe's compound, taking big strides towards his own hut.

The other younger men followed him, each going to his own hut. Then Chiyei came out, looking very tired and walking with a stick. My brother Dike was leading him away. I felt so sorry for Chiyei but when he came closer to us, I could see that he was very much amused by it all.

'I'm quite sure he was not hurt at all,' Ogoli said under her breath.

'No, he was. But I think he had been drinking in your courtyard again,' I told her.

'How are you feeling now, Chiyei?' Ogoli asked him when he came nearer.

'Oh, I'll live. I shall live to marry if not this one, another woman,' Chiyei said.

Encouraged, I asked: 'Who is she, this proud girl?'

My brother Dike gave me a nasty look, very eloquently telling me not to be such a nosey parker. But he need not have bothered; Chiyei could take good care of himself. 'Why tell you who she is when she may still not be our wife,' he replied to my question tactfully.

We heard Mordi calling Chima, Dike, and the others. They all now had their otuogwu outing cloth on. Our mothers came on to our footpath just then, asking what the matter was. Everybody was talking at once. We did not know what the matter was; all we knew was that Chiyei was not as badly hurt as he looked earlier on in the afternoon.

Then after a pause, Mordi said to Ogoli's mother that they were going to tell the bride's family that we, the people of Odanta, did not want her any more. Not if she was going to allow the young men of her umunna to go about fighting people like Chiyei just because he had a bad foot.

I looked at Chiyei, who was still standing by us. He now had the look of a martyr. His head hung to one side and he made whining noises, saying: 'As if I burnt my foot on purpose.' He looked so funny that we did not know whether to laugh with him or laugh at him.

But Chima, Dike, Afam, and the others were going to the bride's village. Chiyei went on reminding them what to say.

'Tell her people that we even have enough akayan to last them all a whole year. Tell them that the biggest python in Ibusa has been skinned just for her benefit. Tell her that the girls of our Odanta are making the best oil-lamps in the whole world for her. . . .'

'Yes,' said Chima, 'we'll tell them that in spite of all that, we don't want her any more. And in the name of our goddess, no one in this town would marry her again.' And they made their way determinedly out of our footpath.

We had finished eating our evening meal and were having a last look at our lamps in Ogugua's mother's hut, when we saw our men coming back in style. They were singing, and their otuogwu had been rolled up showing their loincloths. They each had two bottles of esimesi under their arms.

'We have got ourselves a wife, a bright shining wife, a nice girl, a sensible girl,' they sang. Even the conservative Chima was singing and dancing too.

'I can't believe this,' I yelled.

We ran out of Ogugua's hut to see our young men looking so happy, so noisy and so like our fathers. My father came out and laughed. 'Look at our ambassadors. They have been bribed by the very girl they went to tell off.'

'It was not her fault,' hiccoughed Chima. 'She didn't know when her stupid brothers arranged to go and fight Chiyei. I think she will just suit Chiyei. Girls like her . . . because they are unusual, often bring luck to an umunna. Did we not kill the python, just because of her . . .?'

Chiyei came out from his hut. I could see that he felt hurt that his kinsmen had been given so much to eat and drink on a mission from which he was excluded, just because he happened to be the principal actor.

'The wife is yours now, Chiyei. She will be arriving in style at this umunna on the next Eke day. So, man, go and make yourself ready,' advised Mordi.

But Chiyei's eyes were more on the bottles of esimesi than on anything else. 'Don't finish those drinks,' he warned.

'Are you more concerned about the drink than the fact that a bride has been arranged for you by your kinsmen?'

'Thank you very much for securing the bride for me. But the drinks are equally important.'

Chiyei made as if to get a bottle or two from our tottering ambassadors. But my father was quicker. 'You are still a sick man, Chiyei. Go into your hut and get yourself better. And you young men, go and carry on with the skinning and preparation of the python skin.'

We saw four elderly men walking gravely and yet with an amused air into our umunna.

'Yes, she is a sensible bride. She has even seen to it that her people are sent to ask for forgiveness. All will be well,' said my father.

The Moon is Out!

The moon is out,
The new moon is out,
Come out and play,
The moon is out!

I could tell from where I was sitting on the floor at the back of our hut, eating my evening meal, that the singing voice belonged to Akeje. My first reaction was to jump up and skip out and join the fun of welcoming the new moon. Then my big brother eyed me darkly and warned: 'If you leave now, I will eat all your fish.' This kept me glued to my place as I ate hurriedly. I waited impatiently for my brothers and sister to finish so that I could wash out the soup bowls.

Soon, the solo voice announcing the new moon became the voices of many. I could tell from where I was sitting, impatiently twisting my fingers, that others had joined in. Eventually, I was able to go out and join my friends. We were all jumping and singing, for the moon symbolizes a new beginning for us. The fact that one has been spared the uncertainties of the last month and is alive to herald the beginning of a new one is worth giving thanks for. And like most things, we gave thanks in songs and laughter.

The young boys were happy too. But from childhood, boys were brought up to be more reserved in showing their emotion. They rejoiced quietly and talked in low voices as if they were forever keeping secrets.

After the first greeting of the new moon, I decided to go to the back of our hut to wash my baby sister's sticky fingers. She did not wait to have her hands washed, she simply rushed out with me. We chattered from the front doorway to the door at the back and there we had to stop short, surprised at what we saw.

My mother was standing looking sad, and addressing appeals to the new moon. We could hear her praying to the moon to be kind to us, to send us good health, and to bless the bride that would be coming to our umunna homestead on the morrow. She was completely unaware of us, so preoccupied was she in her prayers.

I took my sister's hands, washed them quietly, and urged her outside, leaving my mother with her thoughts. That sight made me thoughtful for a while, but not for long.

A louder noise attracted my attention. From the court-yard belonging to Obi Ibekwe, Ogoli's father, came young men skipping and shouting. They were holding over their heads what I first took to be the python.

I held my sister tightly and was ready to bolt back into our hut, when I noticed that this python looked weightless. Yes, I could see it now as it came closer. It was the skin of the snake.

'Isn't it beautiful?' I said to Awele, but she did not understand what it all meant. She was sucking her thumb thoughtfully and by the way she was holding me, I knew that she thought it was the real python.

68

'Look, it is the python mat. Look!' I shouted to her excitedly.

Ogoli and Ngua and Akeje soon joined me, and we followed the happy young men in the snake-dance to the open square, just by the entrance to our homestead, called Otinkpu. By the time they reached this place, a large crowd had gathered. Many adults praised the young people's handiwork openly. They had not damaged the skin at all. Many people came from the neighbouring homesteads to congratulate us on our luck in discovering the python before it was able to do any harm. They all agreed that it was the good luck of the bride arriving on the morrow. Chiyei was to be lucky from now on. First he was having a new wife to look after him when everybody had given up hope of his ever marrying again, now our goddess Oboshi had sent this python almost to our door so that its priceless skin could be used by the bride for bearing her babies. Such a lucky bride. Other women delivered their babies on banana leaves, but this one was going to have a priceless mat.

We children were called to sit on the python skin. I was scared at first, because the intricate workings on the skin reminded me so much of the real thing. The boys sat first saying that they hoped our new wife would have seven sons. We all eventually did this amidst great laughter from our parents, who stood by watching and appealing to the new moon not to turn a deaf ear to the prayers of us young children.

We danced back from Otinkpu to Obi Ibekwe's court-yard, carrying the python skin after it had been offered to the moon and blessed.

'Do you know, I can hardly wait to know who the bride is,' said Ogugua, tugging at my arm as we made our way to the back of my mother's hut to finish arranging our lamps ready for the morrow.

'You know, I'm beginning to be uneasy about it, after

hearing what our mothers were saying on their way from the stream last Eke market day. You remember I told you about it. They sounded as if she is different somehow. But how?'

'In any case,' said Ogugua, 'she is capable of having babies, otherwise they wouldn't encourage us to keep the python skin for her. Do you know that that Aba trader who bought the snake's meat was offering to pay ten white man's pounds for it? But the elders refused to sell. They were keeping it specially for Chiyei and his new wife.'

'It's nice to start married life with such wealth and luck. And did you see how beautiful it is? And how beautiful our lamps are? My mother said that they looked better than the professional ones.'

After making sure that the lamps were in a safe place until needed, we skipped into the square to join our friends and age-group in story-telling. We often did this, but especially when there was a new moon.

We would first of all arrange ourselves in a circle, and start to sing and dance to all the fabled songs of our ancestors. One girl would stay in the centre and dance her fill, then another would take over from where she had left. At the end of it, when the square was filled with people, we sat round and listened to old women tell stories of our people of long ago. I personally did not like those long and winding tales told by adults, full of morals about what you have to do and what not to do. But tonight, even Ogoli's mother—who often told the dreariest stories—was inspired to tell humorous ones, spiced with beautiful songs.

As we all went back to our huts after midnight, I could see that all of us could scarcely wait for tomorrow.

11

The Bride Arrives

On the morning of that Eke day when our bride was to arrive, there was mist in the air. But the early morning mist did not dampen our enthusiasm and burning expectation at all. To me in particular, this was one of the rare occasions when I would see a bride arrive in our umunna. The fact that we did not know who the bride was, and the fact that the bride was for Chiyei, heightened the excitement the more.

As I swept out our hut and got ready to go to the stream, I saw my mother folding her special lappas which she kept for occasions like this. She left them in the morning dew to bring out the gloss. Now the mist was giving way to morning sunshine, and as she brought them in, she pampered each in turn as one would a very, very dear child.

The preparation for the bride went on all day in our village. The main footpath was swept clean, and Otinkpu was cleared for dancers. But the greatest change and wonder of all was in Chiyei himself.

He had been an embarrassment to us until recently. On Eke days like this he would go to the stalls of the palm-wine climbers from the East and, without washing himself, he would stay there till midnight. He would then come home carrying bottles of esimesi. And he would sing and dance, then bless himself and condemn himself, all alone. He was so well known in the whole of Ibusa that people would sometimes ask us if we came from the same umunna as the great palm-wine drinker and eater, Chiyei. Whenever there was a gunshot to announce the death of somebody, he would kneel openly and thank his god, because he knew that he would have free palm wine and pounded yam until the person was buried.

His age-group would only tolerate him because they knew that it was unlawful to reject a person of the same age just because he had funny ways. The pity of it was that Chiyei was well aware that he was unwanted. Whenever he stood up to talk, people would shout him down and say 'Sit down, Chiyei, this conversation concerns full men, not half men.' In this way they referred to his wifelessness and childlessness. How could he contribute anything sensible to the pool of ideas when he'd never had children of his own?

But today Chiyei walked so tall and proud that the limp which had been his handicap now became a mark of distinction. He had shaved his head clean and washed himself so thoroughly that the blackness of his skin shone like wood-carving. He now laughed at everything. During the past market days, he had been going to the market to sell the few yams he had managed to produce on his ill-tended farm. He wanted the homecoming of his bride to have a special place in our memory. With the money he got from the sale of his yams he bought a very big goat, with which he surprised us all on this Eke morning.

With the arrival of the goat, the young men were set to work again, killing and flaying. Our mothers had to hurry to the stream for a bath and be back home to do the cooking. Every household contributed yams and fish, and soon many odos could be heard pounding and pounding yams for our guests.

To make sure all would be well, Obi Ibekwe invited the rainmakers from Ezukwu. The man with a head like a gourd came and rattled his charm all day long at Otinkpu. With him there, we were sure there would be no rain that day. It didn't rain at all, that day or for many days after.

I could not remember any other day in which we made so many trips to the stream; so much water was needed for the cooking and washing. And there was so much to eat and taste. After each trip to the stream we were rewarded with pieces of fried meat and dry fish, all soaked in palm-oil, with crusty yam. I was full even before the evening arrived.

The first group to arrive made my heart sink a little. I was still tying my festive lappa when there was a burst of laughter, very near where the rainmaker was still working. I ran out, and saw a group of twenty or so men, all dressed in their festive lappas, clapping and doing some mock-bridal steps. They were addressing Chiyei in his praise-name and telling him in songs that he had been eating other people's food, but today they were here to eat his food and drink his palm wine and see his bride. They were his eating companions, of course.

I ran to my mother and said in a whisper: 'Look, Mother, they will eat all the food.' There was such a panic in my voice that Ogugua's mother laughed when she heard me. I was assured that they would not. For not only were they cooking Chiyei's goat and pounding hundreds of yams, but the goat bought with the python-meat money was cooked and ready to drink palm wine with.

We the daughters of our homesteads soon found places for them to sit, on benches specially constructed with bamboo. Large kegs of palm wine arrived and hundreds of kola nuts and meat. The men started to sing and dance in their own funny fashion. Soon Chiyei's age-group dancers arrived, and after that I lost count of who was arriving and who was leaving.

Different sets of people danced until it was night and the moon came out once more. Our parents arranged us in age-groups. My group was the youngest, so they arranged us in the front. The others stood behind in age order. The very old men and women stayed at home to receive the bride when she arrived, and to entertain our dancing visitors. Only the people of our umunna were qualified to go, yet what a big crowd we made. Then Ogoli brought out our lamps and people shouted, admiring their beauty and praising our handiwork.

We could not start the bridal song, because we did not know the name of the bride. Then Afam, the young and intense son of Mordi, started from the back with his rich male voice and sang:

> 'Ugbo ebule, eee
> Ugbo ebule Ototo eee
> Ototo ma nma, Ima na osi na Lego bia.'

'Ototo, who is Ototo?' we asked each other, looking rather amused. 'How can somebody's name be Ototo? Ototo are flowers.'

Still, we started to sing with him. The men beat their gongs, the women shook their beaded gourds, and those behind us clapped their hands and some even knocked spoons on esimesi bottles. We danced on the spot for a few minutes before we progressed slowly towards Omeze, another cluster of homesteads not too far from us. As we neared the village, Afam the soloist changed from calling our bride Ototo, which he said in his song that we were coming to take away in a beautiful boat, and started to call her 'Alatiriki'.

Here we were really baffled. But we could ask no question. We just answered the chorus in the words he had

74

chosen. First our new bride was referred to as flowers, now she was called 'Electricity'.

'She must be a very fair person,' Ogoli said to me in a stage whisper.

I nodded in the dim light, and laughed at the same time.

We were soon put out of our wondering as we neared Omeze. The dancers and singers for no reason at all became more intense in their performance. We simply followed their example. Then suddenly they stopped in front of a big hut, belonging to the oldest Obi of that village. A group of dancers came from that hut to meet us and it became a gay, almost riotous party. We knew then that we had arrived at the family hut of our bride. It was then I started to suspect who our bride could be, because there was only one girl in this hut, and I'd met her many a time at our stream in Atakpo.

'I think we are marrying an albino,' giggled Ogoli.

'Keep quiet, it may be a relative of hers, but if it's Echi, do you mind very much?' I asked.

'No, I don't mind. She can't help being an albino, but what made me laugh a little is the way Afam insisted on referring to her as "Alatiriki".'

'It's supposed to be a pet name. It means she is so fair that she will lighten up our umunna like electricity which our relatives who live in the city talk about every time they come home on a visit.'

'She is coming out. But look, she is beautiful tonight. They have really made her up. Let us go and bid her welcome with our lamps.'

As we rushed forward to take our bride from her people, the oldest Obi in her cluster of homesteads shot a gun into the air, telling the whole of Ibusa that a well-beloved daughter was leaving her people. With this, the women in her family started to cry and were showering her with chalk, a symbol of fertility. They were losing her, but we were happy because she was now ours.

As we got her on our side, our best dancers and acrobats performed many wonders, before the men in our group thanked the parents of the bride. There was a long reply, after which we were all given some home-made gin, and were permitted to take our 'Alatiriki' wife home. As soon as this was complete, Chima performed what looked like magic before our eyes. From somewhere among them, he suddenly unrolled the python skin. It was done so cleverly that in the dim light provided by our lamps and the moon it looked as if we had conjured a snake. There was a great gasp as people ran for cover. We from Odanta laughed, and ordered our new wife to kneel on it as we danced round. It was such an impressive performance, and I could see that our new wife, Echi, was proud of us.

After more dances, our young men took all the bride things, at the same time murmuring thanks to her people for being so generous, because they really bought her so many household things. She had expensive-looking mats, many bales of abada material, beautiful clay pots and even iron cooking-pots. It took ten of our men to carry them all. When they had balanced all these things on their shoulders we surrounded our bride and held our lamps high, as we burst into song again:

>Ugbo ebule Alatiriki ooooo
>Ima na osi na Lego bia

which in English means

>A boat is carrying our Electricity of a bride,
>Our bride who came for Lagos.

For our bride responded warmly to all our efforts to make her feel welcome, so much so that we all forgot that she was an albino.

The merriment went on for many days. As for that night,

76

the moon shone as if it would never stop, and our Electricity of a wife—later known as 'Alatiriki'—glowed from under her silk scarf.

One thing nearly spoiled it all for us—the bridegroom. He completely forgot that it was his bride that was coming home, and drank too much palm wine with his drinking friends. He even competed in the pounded yam competition, and almost won. He came second as the greatest fast eater in the whole of Ibusa town.

Our mother ignored Chiyei. She washed and dressed the bride for the night and sat her on the special mat made from the python skin.

Alatiriki, our fair wife, stayed with us and, less than a year later, used that very python mat for delivering her first baby boy. And even though he was fair, he was not an albino like the mother. Our Alatiriki put up with our Chiyei, and persuaded him to be a little more responsible. He still ate a lot and drank too much, but he knew that now he had a wife and a child to care for. They had many more children, none of them albino, but our people say that at some future date those children could have albino babies.

Well, we did not mind. Our Alatiriki of a wife had the best sense of humour in all our umunna, and she taught us it matters little the colour or superficial beauty of any person, the most important thing is the beauty of the heart. And our wife Echi, or Alatiriki, had that.

I was happy I went to the banana grove with Ogoli on that Eke day to get clay for the lamps to welcome such a wonderful person into our umunna, Odanta.